Where is Jumper?

Ellen
Stoll
Walsh

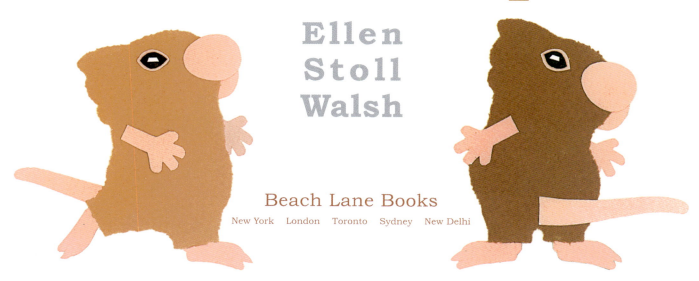

Beach Lane Books

New York   London   Toronto   Sydney   New Delhi

BEACH LANE BOOKS
An imprint of Simon & Schuster Children's Publishing Division
1230 Avenue of the Americas, New York, New York 10020
Beach Lane Books is a trademark of Simon & Schuster, Inc.
For information about special discounts for bulk purchases, please contact
Simon & Schuster Special Sales at 1-866-506-1949 or business@simonandschuster.com.
The Simon & Schuster Speakers Bureau can bring authors to your live event.
For more information or to book an event, contact the Simon & Schuster Speakers
Bureau at 1-866-248-3049 or visit our website at www.simonspeakers.com.
The text for this book is set in Bookman Old Style.
The illustrations for this book are rendered in collage.
Manufactured in China
0715 SCP
First Edition
10 9 8 7 6 5 4 3 2 1
Library of Congress Cataloging-in-Publication Data
Walsh, Ellen Stoll, author, illustrator.
Where is Jumper? / Ellen Stoll Walsh.—First edition.
p. cm.
Summary: Jumper is missing, and his mouse friends look for him inside the cave and
outside, up among the branches and down into mole's tunnel, but still they cannot
find him.
ISBN 978-1-4814-4508-5 (hardback)
ISBN 978-1-4814-4509-2 (eBook)
[1. Hide-and-seek—Fiction. 2. English language—Prepositions—Fiction. 3. Mice—Fiction.]
I. Title.
PZ7.W1675Whe 2015
[E]—dc23
2015005164

For the real Theodore

Для настоящего Теодора

The mice climbed over
and around the rocks . . .

and ran across a log, one in front of the other.

But somewhere between the log and the pond, Jumper disappeared!

The mice looked for him inside the cave . . .

and outside . . .

and below
the fallen tree.

They looked up,
among the branches . . .

and down,
into Mole's tunnel.

Here's Mole! But still no Jumper.

What if the sneaky weasel got him?

Oh no!

Then, something moved underneath the leaves, and . . .

out popped Jumper!

And off he went,
through the woods.

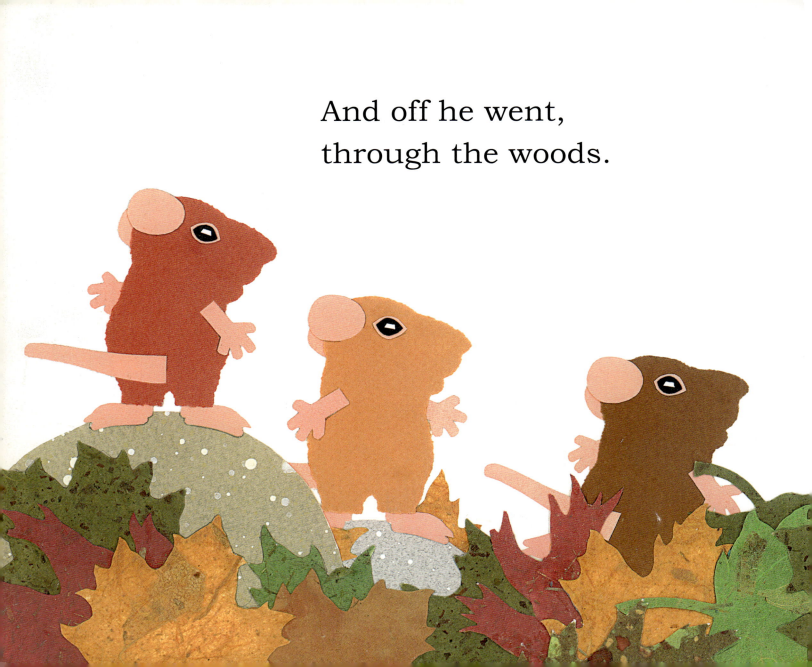

Now where is Jumper?

Here he is!

But where is everyone else?